Zoom Squirrel

Bam Squirrel

Flappy Squirrel

Norman

Zing Squirrel

Klink Squirrel

Wink Squirrel

Happy Squirrel

HYPERION BOOKS FOR CHILDREN / *NEW YORK*

For Tracey!

Look, **Zowie Squirrel**!

I found a **Sable** of Contents!

Hi!

That might have to do, **Wowie Squirrel**, because the **Table of Contents** is missing!

Don't worry. I have the **order** of the stories right here!

Look for the **EMOTE-ACORNS** in this story.

They pop up when the Squirrels have **BIG** feelings!

HAPPY

EXCITED

SCARED

FRUSTRATED

SAD

CONFUSED

The BIG Story!

By **Mo Willems**

Hi, **Zoom Squirrel!**

Hi, **Squirrel Friends**!

WE HAVE FEELINGS!

And we want to share some with you.

That makes me feel **happy**!

First feeling is on the house.

Cool.

Would you like **another feeling**?

YES! I WOULD LIKE TO TRY A **NEW FEELING**!

Let's see . . .

Have you ever been **disappointed**?

I am not sure.

14

DISAPPOINT ME!!!

I am ready
to be
disappointed.

feelings

Now.

You have to make a **disappointment appointment**.

That makes me feel . . .

Well . . .

Uh . . .

I do not have a **word** for it.

Maybe we can offer you—

a **different** feeling?

Okay.

Frustration?

Hmm . . .

Okay.

Frustrate me!

Bad news, **Zoomy**.

We **cannot** frustrate you.

You do not have **any** frustration. . . .

Then WHY
offer it

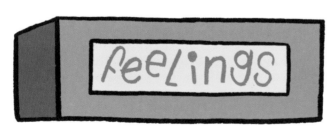

feelings

did you
to me!?!

COME **ON**!

First you cannot **disappoint** me!

Then you cannot **frustrate** me!

That makes me

so . . . .

so . . . .

so . . . .

GRRRRR

RRR
PRR

RRRRRRRR
RRRRR
RRRRR!

Do you have **another feeling** in stock right now that I can feel **instead** of this?

We **found** something.

What is
this **old
feeling**?

LOVE!

Well, I **learned** something today.

Squirrels **may not know** a lot about every feeling.

But they **do know** how to be **great friends**.

That was a **funny** story with a **happy** ending!

Yup.

It's ACORN-Y JOKE TIME!

100% CORNY!

59

NOTHING!

Rocks **cannot talk!**

Really?

Roll with it!

The joke is over.

Is it **my turn** now?

Not yet.

It is **their turn** now!

Research Rodent here to ask some Squirrel Friends a **question**!

What do you do when you get **frustrated**?

I take a **deep breath**.

I try to solve my problem in a **new way**.

I count my **lucky stars**.

What do **you** do when you get frustrated, **Research Rodent**?

Research with my friends!

I am starting to
get **frustrated**. . . .

Maybe **another
Acorn-y Joke** will help.

It's **ACORN-Y JOKE TIME!**

71.49% CORNY!

Okay, **Hey-Corn.** What did the **rock who could talk** say to the **other rock who could talk?**

I got this!

NOTHING!!!

The rocks were **shy**!

I'm **rocking** your world!

73

One more
Acorn-y Joke,
Happy Squirrel!

Hey-Corn!

Hi-Corn!

It's ACORN-Y JOKE TIME!

3% CORNY!

Oooo-kay!
What did the **talking rock, who was not shy,** say to the **other not-shy talking rock?**

Easy!

NOTHING!!!

This joke took so long, the rocks **went to bed**!

Grrrrr!

Never take a punch line for **granite**!

Your turn, **Happy Squirrel**!

What did you want to say?

I WANTED TO SAY THAT SOMETIMES YOU CAN BE HAPPY!!!

Good for you!
You **said it**!

I did?

Just now.

I did!

THAT MAKES

This book is set in Avenir LT Pro/Monotype; Minion Pro, Billy/Fontspring; Typography of Coop,
Fink, Neutraface/House Industries

Printed in the United States of America
Reinforced binding

First Edition, September 2022
10 9 8 7 6 5 4 3 2 1
FAC-034274-21232

Library of Congress Cataloging-in-Publication Data

Names: Willems, Mo, author, illustrator.
Title: The frustrating book! / by Mo Willems.
Description: First edition. • New York, New York : Hyperion Books for
    Children, 2022. • Series: Unlimited squirrels • Audience: Ages 4–8. •
    Audience: Grades 2–3. • Summary: Squirrel friends introduce some new
    emotions to Zoom Squirrel.
Identifiers: LCCN 2022009469 • ISBN 9781368074827 (hardback)
Subjects: CYAC: Emotions—Fiction. • Squirrels—Fiction. • Humorous
    stories. • LCGFT: Picture books.
Classification: LCC PZ7.W65535 Fr 2022 • DDC [E]—dc23
LC record available at https://lccn.loc.gov/2022009469

Visit www.hyperionbooksforchildren.com and www.pigeonpresents.com

Hey!

Why didn't I
get to be in the
main book!?!